Dear Parents:

D0453761

Congratulations! Your child is taking the first steps on an exciting journey. The destination? Independent reading!

STEP INTO READING® will help your child get there. The program offers five steps to reading success. Each step includes fun stories and colorful art or photographs. In addition to original fiction and books with favorite characters, there are Step into Reading Non-Fiction Readers, Phonics Readers and Boxed Sets, Sticker Readers, and Comic Readers—a complete literacy program with something to interest every child.

Learning to Read, Step by Step!

Ready to Read   Preschool–Kindergarten
• big type and easy words • rhyme and rhythm • picture clues
For children who know the alphabet and are eager to begin reading.

Reading with Help   Preschool–Grade 1
• basic vocabulary • short sentences • simple stories
For children who recognize familiar words and sound out new words with help.

Reading on Your Own   Grades 1–3
• engaging characters • easy-to-follow plots • popular topics
For children who are ready to read on their own.

Reading Paragraphs   Grades 2–3
• challenging vocabulary • short paragraphs • exciting stories
For newly independent readers who read simple sentences with confidence.

Ready for Chapters   Grades 2–4
• chapters • longer paragraphs • full-color art
For children who want to take the plunge into chapter books but still like colorful pictures.

STEP INTO READING® is designed to give every child a successful reading experience. The grade levels are only guides; children will progress through the steps at their own speed, developing confidence in their reading. The F&P Text Level on the back cover serves as another tool to help you choose the right book for your child.

Remember, a lifetime love of reading starts with a single step!

For Dash, Jules, and Kaizen
—D.U.

For Jake and my family, who have
never stopped believing in me
—K.M.

Text copyright © 2023 by Deborah Underwood
Cover art and interior illustrations copyright © 2023 by Kaley McCabe

All rights reserved. Published in the United States by Random House Children's Books, a division of Penguin Random House LLC, New York.

Step into Reading, Random House, and the Random House colophon are registered trademarks of Penguin Random House LLC.

Visit us on the Web!
rhcbooks.com

Educators and librarians, for a variety of teaching tools, visit us at RHTeachersLibrarians.com

Library of Congress Cataloging-in-Publication Data
Names: Underwood, Deborah, author. | McCabe, Kaley, illustrator.
Title: Once upon a zombie : tales for brave readers / by Deborah Underwood ; illustrated by Kaley McCabe.
Description: First edition. | New York : Random House Children's Books, [2023] | Series: Step into reading. Step 3 | Audience: Ages 5–8. | Summary: A child lulls an attacking zombie with undead-themed fairy tales.
Identifiers: LCCN 2022022937 (print) | LCCN 2022022938 (ebook) |
ISBN 978-0-593-57139-2 (trade paperback) | ISBN 978-0-593-57140-8 (library binding) |
ISBN 978-0-593-57141-5 (ebook)
Subjects: LCSH: Children's stories, American. | Zombies—Juvenile fiction. |
CYAC: Zombies—Fiction. | Bedtime—Fiction. | Fairy tales—Adaptations. | Short stories. |
LCGFT: Short stories. | Zombie fiction.
Classification: LCC PZ7.U4193 On 2023 (print) | LCC PZ7.U4193 (ebook) | DDC [Fic]—dc23

Printed in the United States of America
10 9 8 7 6 5 4 3 2 1
First Edition

This book has been officially leveled by using the F&P Text Level Gradient™ Leveling System.

Once Upon a
ZOMBIE

TALES FOR BRAVE READERS

by Deborah Underwood
illustrated by Kaley McCabe

Random House 🏠 New York

What if

you were sleeping

in the middle of the night . . .

and a ZOMBIE crashed

through your window?

Would you run?

Would you scream?

Would you hide?

Of course not.

You're smart.

You know zombies don't

always want to

eat your brains.

Sometimes they just want

a bedtime story.

Here's one. . . .

Little Red Zombie

Once upon a time,
Little Red Zombie
went to visit her granny.

As Little Red skipped
through the forest,
a big bad wolf
jumped out.
"What's in your basket,
little girl?" he asked.

"Brains for
my granny's breakfast!"
said Little Red Zombie.

The wolf didn't believe her.

Who would take brains

to her granny?

(Hint: A zombie, that's who!)

"What is *really*

in your basket?" the wolf asked.

"Brains!" Little Red Zombie said

as she skipped past him.

The hungry wolf was
very curious.
What was she hiding
in the basket?

11

A cake?

A pumpkin pie?

It must be something yummy.

He would eat it

for breakfast.

Then he would eat

the little girl for dessert!

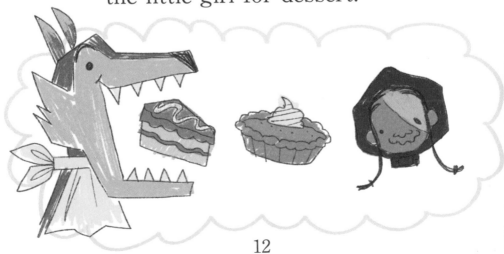

The wolf took a shortcut
through the woods.

Little Red Zombie arrived
at Granny's house.
But Granny looked different.

Her eyeballs weren't
falling out of their sockets.
Her ears weren't
dangling off her head.
Her teeth weren't bloody red.

15

"Granny, what normal eyes
you have!" said Little Red.

"The better to see you with,
my dear," replied the wolf.

"Granny, what normal ears
you have!" said Little Red.

"The better to hear you with,
my dear," replied the wolf.

"Granny, what normal teeth
you have!" said Little Red.

"The better to eat
what's in that basket,
my dear!" cried the wolf.

He sprang out of bed.

He grabbed Little Red's basket.

He lifted up the cloth . . .

and screamed.

Just then, Granny crashed

through the wall.

"How lovely!

A basket of brains!

And fresh wolf brains

for dessert!" Granny said.

"My favorite!"

The wolf ran away
as fast as his hairy legs
could carry him.

Is your zombie asleep yct?

No?

Then here's another story.

Hansel and Gretel Zombie

One day, a mean lady sent
Hansel and Gretel Zombie
into the woods.
She hoped they would
get lost forever.

But they were smart.
They dropped
a trail of eyeballs
behind them.
They would
follow the eyeballs
to get back home.

But a zombie raven
ate all the eyeballs!

"Now what?" asked
Hansel Zombie.
"I'm so hungry!" said
Gretel Zombie.

They saw a house.
The house was covered
with cookies and candies.

"Cookies and candies? Ick,"
said Gretel Zombie.
"It's better than nothing,"
said Hansel Zombie.
They began to eat.

Inside the house,

a witch said,

"Nibble, nibble, little mouse.

Who is nibbling at my house?"

There was no answer.

"I know who eats cookies

and candies . . .

children do!" said the witch.

(Hint: So do zombies,

if they are hungry enough.)

"I will have children soup

for lunch!"

She put a big pot on the fire.

She flung open the door.

"Come in, dear children!"

she called.

The witch looked up
from her pot . . .
and screamed.

"Witch brains for lunch!"

Gretel Zombie said.

"My favorite!" said Hansel.

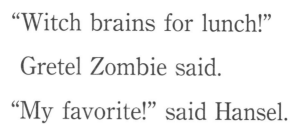

The witch ran away
as fast as her hairy legs
could carry her.

Now is your zombie asleep?

No?

Goodness!

All right, then.

One last story.

Three Little Zombies

The big bad wolf was tired.

He'd had a hard day.

So he went to find dinner.

He saw a straw house,

a stick house,

and a brick house.

"The Three Little Pigs

must live here,"

the wolf said.

"Who else would have

houses like that?"

(Hint: The Three Little Zombies,

silly wolf!)

The wolf knocked

on the first Little Zombie's door.

There was no answer.

So he huffed and he puffed,

and he blew the house down.

No one was inside!

But the wolf found

something strange.

"Why would a pig have
a can of brains
in the kitchen?"
he wondered.

The wolf knocked
on the second
Little Zombie's door.

There was no answer.

So he huffed and he puffed,

and he blew the house down.

No one was inside!
But the wolf found
something strange.

"Why would a pig have
The Brains Cookbook?"
he wondered.

The wolf knocked
on the third
Little Zombie's door.

"There must be a pig
somewhere in this story,"
he said.

The door flew open.

The Three Little Zombies

grinned at him.

"Wolf brains for dinner!" said

the Three Little Zombies.

"Our favorite!"

The wolf ran away
as fast as his hairy legs
could carry him.

The wolf met the witch

at the bakery.

They ordered pumpkin muffins.

"Would you like brains with that?"

asked the Zombie Muffin Man.

"NO," the wolf and the witch
said together.

"Storybook Land is going downhill,"
the wolf said.

"I'm moving to Nebraska."

"Me too," said the witch.

Is your zombie asleep yet?

Yes? Good!

Now get out of there.

When zombies wake up,

they are usually very

HUNGRY!